PAT HUTCHINS
SHRINKING MOUSE

Greenwillow Books New York

Gouache paints were used for the full-color art.
The text type is Symbol ITC Medium.

Printed in Hong Kong by South China Printing
Company (1988) Ltd.
First Edition   10   9   8   7   6   5   4   3   2   1

Library of Congress Cataloging-in-Publication Data

Hutchins, Pat (date)
Shrinking mouse / by Pat Hutchins.
       p.   cm.
Summary: Four animal friends notice that
the size of distant objects seems to change
depending on the location and movement
of the viewer.
ISBN 0-688-13961-2 (trade)
ISBN 0-688-13962-0 (lib. bdg.)
[1. Size—Fiction.   2. Animals—Fiction.
3. Visual perception—Fiction.]   I. Title.
PZ7.H96165Sf   1997   [E]—dc20
96-5393   CIP   AC

For Les
and
Mary Beckett

Fox, Rabbit, Squirrel, and Mouse
were sitting at the edge of their
wood, looking across the fields.
"Look at that tiny wood over there,"
said Mouse. "It's even smaller than
I am. And look, there's Owl flying
toward it."

"Oh, dear!" said Fox. "He's shrinking. I'll go and tell him to come back before he disappears altogether." And Fox set out after Owl.

"Oh, dear!" cried Rabbit. "Fox is shrinking, too. I'll go and tell him to come back before he disappears like Owl!"
And Rabbit set off after Fox.

"Oh, dear!" cried Squirrel.
"Rabbit is shrinking, too!
  I'll go and tell him to come back
  before he disappears like Fox!"
  And Squirrel set off after Rabbit.

Poor Mouse was very upset.
"Squirrel is shrinking, as well!" he
thought. "I must try and stop him
before he disappears like the rest
of my friends."
And Mouse scampered after Squirrel.

"The wood is getting bigger," thought Mouse. "I must be shrinking, too!" Poor Mouse didn't want to be any smaller, but he kept on running.

"The wood is really big now," thought Mouse. "I must have nearly disappeared!" Mouse didn't want to disappear, but he kept on running.

And when he got to the wood, there were Owl and all his friends.

"Have I disappeared?" asked Mouse.

"No," they said. "You're just the right size!"

"Good," said Mouse. "Let's go home." But when he turned to look at their wood, it was very, very small.

"Oh," Mouse cried. "Our wood has shrunk, too! We can't go home!"

"Follow me," said Owl.
So they did.

And as they got closer
to their wood, it got bigger. . .

and bigger.

"Are we getting smaller?" asked Mouse.

"No," said Owl as they reached their wood. "We're all just the right size."

And he flew away.

"Oh, dear!" said Fox.
"Owl is shrinking again."
"Don't worry," said Mouse.
"I'm sure he'll be the right size
   when he comes back."

And he was.

DATE DUE